ROALD DAHL'S

BEWARE THE WITCHES!

A STICKER AND ACTIVITY BOOK

illustrated by Quentin Blake

GROSSET & DUNLAP
An Imprint of Penguin Random House

GROSSET & DUNLAP

Penguin Young Readers Group
An Imprint of Penguin Random House LLC

Additional text by Hannah S. Campbell

Text copyright © 1983, 2016 by Roald Dahl Nominee Ltd. Illustrations copyright © 1983 by Quentin Blake. All rights reserved. Published in 2016 by Grosset & Dunlap, an imprint of Penguin Random House LLC, 345 Hudson Street, New York, New York 10014. GROSSET & DUNLAP is a trademark of Penguin Random House LLC. Manufactured in China.

ISBN 9781101996003   10 9 8 7 6 5 4 3 2 1

BEWARE THE WITCHES

In fairy-tales, witches always wear silly black hats and black cloaks, and they ride on broomsticks.

But this is not a fairy-tale. This is about **REAL WITCHES**.

I myself had two separate encounters with witches before I was eight years old.

From the first I escaped unharmed, but on the second occasion I was not so lucky.

Things happened to me that will probably make you scream when you read about them.

That can't be helped. The truth must be told.

GRANDMOTHER

The fact that I am still here and able to speak to you (however peculiar I may look) is due entirely to my wonderful grandmother.

My grandmother was Norwegian. This old lady, as far as I could gather, was just about the only surviving relative we had on either side of our family. She was my mother's mother and I absolutely adored her. When she and I were together we spoke in either Norwegian or in English. It didn't matter which. We were equally fluent in both languages, and I have to admit that I felt closer to her than to my mother.

Name somebody who is very special to you.

bro, mom, dad, grandma/pa, Justin, Alisson
bradly

When and how did you meet this person?

I met mom by the mom first time eat I ng
it was burn

List three things you like about them.

1. buy me everything

2. there fun

3. They care about me

Tell the story of one of your favorite memories with this person.

I drowning with my cosin Justi,
Alisson and grampa,

What gift would this person enjoy more than anything else?

A hug

5

WHAT ARE WITCHES?

REAL WITCHES dress in ordinary clothes and look very much like ordinary women. They live in ordinary houses and they work in **ORDINARY JOBS**.

That is why they are so hard to catch.

A **REAL WITCH** hates children with a red-hot sizzling hatred that is more sizzling and red-hot than any hatred you could possibly imagine.

A **REAL WITCH** spends all her time plotting to get rid of the children in her particular territory. Her passion is to do away with them, one by one. It is all she thinks about the whole day long. Even if she is working as a cashier in a supermarket or typing letters for a businessman or driving round in a fancy car (and she could be doing any of these things), her mind will always be plotting and scheming and churning and burning and whizzing and phizzing with murderous bloodthirsty thoughts.

WITCHY WORD SEARCH

Find as many of these witchy words as you can:

- witchophile
- gloves
- blue spit
- bald
- frizzled

- nitrash
- claws
- nose-holes
- stink-waves
- eyes

- square feet
- The Grand High Witch
- Mouse-Maker
- castle
- squelched

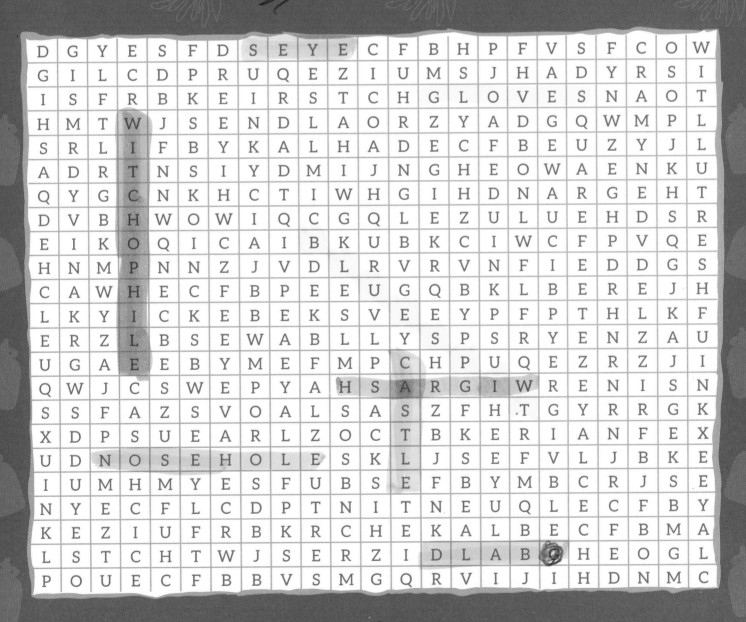

D	G	Y	E	S	F	D	S	E	Y	E	C	F	B	H	P	F	V	S	F	C	O	W
G	I	L	C	D	P	R	U	Q	E	Z	I	U	M	S	J	H	A	D	Y	R	S	I
I	S	F	R	B	K	E	I	R	S	T	C	H	G	L	O	V	E	S	N	A	O	T
H	M	T	W	J	S	E	N	D	L	A	O	R	Z	Y	A	D	G	Q	W	M	P	L
S	R	L	I	F	B	Y	K	A	L	H	A	D	E	C	F	B	E	U	Z	Y	J	L
A	D	R	T	N	S	I	Y	D	M	I	J	N	G	H	E	O	W	A	E	N	K	U
Q	Y	G	C	N	K	H	C	T	I	W	H	G	I	H	D	N	A	R	G	E	H	T
D	V	B	H	W	O	W	I	Q	C	G	Q	L	E	Z	U	L	U	E	H	D	S	R
E	I	K	O	Q	I	C	A	I	B	K	U	B	K	C	I	W	C	F	P	V	Q	E
H	N	M	P	N	N	Z	J	V	D	L	R	V	R	V	N	F	I	E	D	D	G	S
C	A	W	H	E	C	F	B	P	E	E	U	G	Q	B	K	L	B	E	R	E	J	H
L	K	Y	I	C	K	E	B	E	K	S	V	E	E	Y	P	F	P	T	H	L	K	F
E	R	Z	L	B	S	E	W	A	B	L	L	Y	S	P	S	R	Y	E	N	Z	A	U
U	G	A	E	E	B	Y	M	E	F	M	P	C	H	P	U	Q	E	Z	R	Z	J	I
Q	W	J	C	S	W	E	P	Y	A	H	S	A	R	G	I	W	R	E	N	I	S	N
S	S	F	A	Z	S	V	O	A	L	S	A	S	Z	F	H	T	G	Y	R	R	G	K
X	D	P	S	U	E	A	R	L	Z	O	C	T	B	K	E	R	I	A	N	F	E	X
U	D	N	O	S	E	H	O	L	E	S	K	L	J	S	E	F	V	L	J	B	K	E
I	U	M	H	M	Y	E	S	F	U	B	S	E	F	B	Y	M	B	C	R	I	S	E
N	Y	E	C	F	L	C	D	P	T	N	I	T	N	E	U	Q	L	E	C	F	B	Y
K	E	Z	I	U	F	R	B	K	R	C	H	E	K	A	L	B	E	C	F	B	M	A
L	S	T	C	H	T	W	J	S	E	R	Z	I	D	L	A	B	G	H	E	O	G	L
P	O	U	E	C	F	B	B	V	S	M	G	Q	R	V	I	J	I	H	D	N	M	C

HOW TO SPOT A WITCH

As far as children are concerned, a **REAL WITCH** is easily the most dangerous of all the living creatures on earth. What makes her doubly dangerous is the fact that she doesn't *look* dangerous. Even when you know all the secrets (you will hear about those in a minute), you can still never be sure whether it is a witch you are gazing at or just a kind lady.

Use your stickers to match the different features of REAL WITCHES **to the descriptions!**

A **REAL WITCH** is certain always to be wearing gloves when you meet her. Instead of finger-nails, she has thin curvy claws, like a cat, and she wears the gloves to hide them.

A **REAL WITCH** is always bald. Bald as a boiled egg. A **REAL WITCH** always wears a wig to hide her baldness. And the underneath of a wig is always very rough and scratchy. It sets up a frightful itch on the bald skin. It causes nasty sores on the head. Wig-rash, the witches call it.

Witches have slightly larger nose-holes than ordinary people. The rim of each nose-hole is pink and curvy, like the rim of a certain kind of seashell.

Witches never have toes. They just have feet. The feet have square ends with no toes on them at all.

Their spit is blue. Blue as a bilberry. It is exactly like ink. They even use it to write with. They use those old-fashioned pens that have nibs and they simply lick the nib.

Look in the middle of each eye where there is normally a little black dot. If she is a witch, the black dot will keep changing color, and you will see fire and you will see ice dancing right in the very center of the colored dot.

You can still never be absolutely sure whether a woman is a witch or not just by looking at her. But if she is wearing the gloves, if she has the large nose-holes, the queer eyes, and the hair that looks as though it might be a wig, and if she has a blueish tinge on her teeth—if she has all of these things, then you run like mad.

DOGS' DROPPINGS!
POO-OO-OO-OO!

An absolutely clean child gives off the most ghastly stench to a witch. The smell that drives a witch mad actually comes right out of your own skin. It comes oozing out of your skin in waves, and these waves, stink-waves the witches call them, go floating through the air and hit the witch right smack in her nostrils. They send her reeling. To a witch you'd be smelling of *fresh* dogs' droppings.

What smells do you love? What smells do you find completely disgusting?

BEST SMELLS

Kit kat

me

perfum

WORST SMELLS

pup

PUPlic bathroons

MY FIRST WITCH

A child never forgets his or her first encounter with a witch. It is utterly terrifying, no matter how prepared you are.

I worked away, nailing the first plank on the roof. Then suddenly, out of the corner of my eye, I caught sight of a woman standing immediately below me. She was looking up at me and smiling in the most peculiar way.

I noticed that she was wearing a small black hat and she had black gloves on her hands and the gloves came nearly up to her elbows.

Gloves! She was wearing *gloves!*

I froze all over.

Draw a picture of the witch underneath my tree house!

CLOSE ENCOUNTERS WITH WITCHES!

There are a number of children who have vanished off the face of the earth after crossing paths with witches. In some cases, the children disappeared in very strange ways. But what happened to them afterward?

BIRGIT

Birgit lived just across the road from us. One day she started growing feathers all over her body. Within a month, she had turned into a large white chicken. Her parents kept her for years in a pen in the garden. She even laid eggs.

What did Birgit think about while she was a chicken?

LEIF

A nine-year-old boy called Leif was summer-holidaying with his family on the fjord. Young Leif dived into the water and his father, who was watching him, noticed that he stayed under for an unusually long time. When he came to the surface at last, he wasn't Leif any more. He was a lovely young porpoise. And as friendly as could be. Leif the Porpoise stayed with them all that afternoon giving his brothers and sisters rides on his back. They had a wonderful time. Then he waved a flipper at them and swam away, never to be seen again.

Where did Leif the Porpoise go after he left his family? What did he do?

A GHASTLY SIGHT

As you know, most witches can pass as normal women with just a wig, gloves, and some pointed shoes. But The Grand High Witch's face is so horrendous that she must wear a mask just to be able to go out in public.

Use the masks on the next two pages to disguise yourself as The Grand High Witch—with either of her faces!

Cut out the reversible mask shape, or trace the shape onto a separate piece of paper. On one side, draw The Grand High Witch's mask with a kind, pretty face. On the other side, draw her actual face: rotten and disgusting. Then thread ribbon or elastic through the holes on either side, adjusting for fit as needed. Now you're ready to deceive—or terrify—anyone you meet!

16

FORMULA 86 DELAYED ACTION MOUSE-MAKER

The Grand High Witch has created an awful concoction called Formula 86 Delayed Action Mouse-Maker. She tells the witches to fill chocolates with her formula, then to sell the treats to children. The next morning at school, all the children will turn into mice!

Use your stickers to match all the ingredients of Formula 86 Delayed Action Mouse-Maker:

The wrong end of a telescope, boiled until it is soft

Forty-five brown mouse tails fried in hair-oil until crisp

Frog juice, used to simmer forty-five brown mouse bodies (without tails)

An alarm clock, set for nine o'clock in the morning and roasted until crisp and tender

The yolk of one gruntle's egg

The snout of a grobblesquirt

The claw of a crabcruncher

The tongue of a catspringer

The beak of a blabbersnitch

A GHASTLY SIGHT

Above all the noise, I heard the voice of The Grand High Witch screaming out some sort of an awful gloating song.

Use your word stickers to fill in the blanks!

"Down vith _____ ! Do them in!

Boil their bones and _____ their skin!

Bish them, _____ , bash them, mash them!

Brrreak them, shake them, slash them, smash them!

Offer chocs with _____ !

Say _____ then say it louder.

Crrram them full of sticky eats,

Send them home still _____ .

And in the morning little fools

Go marching off to separate _____ .

A girl feels sick and goes all pale.

She yells, 'Hey look! I've grrrown a tail!'

A boy who's standing next to her

Screams, 'Help! I think I'm _____ !'

Another shouts, 'Vee look like _____ !

There's _____ growing on our cheeks!'

A boy who vos extremely tall

Cries out, 'Vot's wrong? I'm grrrowing small!'

Four _____ begin to sprrrout

From everybody rrround about.

And all at vunce, all in _____ ,

There are no children! Only _____ !

In every school is mice galore

All rrrunning rrround the _____ floor!

And all the poor demented _____

Is yelling, 'Hey, who are these crrreatures?'

They stand upon the desks and shout,

'_____ , you filthy mice! Get out!

Vill someone fetch some _____ , please!

And don't forrrget to bring the _____ !'

Now mouse-trrraps come and every trrrap

Goes _____ and *snappy-snap*.

The mouse-trrraps have a powerful spring,

The springs go _____ and ping!

Is lovely noise for us to hear!

Is music to a _____ !

Dead mice is every place arrround,

Piled _____ deep upon the grrround,

Vith teachers searching left and rrright,

But not a single child in sight!

The teachers cry, '_____

Oh vhere have all the children gone?

Is _____ and as a rrrule

They're never late as this for school!'

Poor teachers don't know vot to do.

Some sit and _____ , and just a few

Amuse themselves throughout the day

By sveeping all the mice avay.

AND ALL US VITCHES _____ !"

LIFE AS A MOUSE

When the witches turned me into a mouse, it took a little getting used to. But should the worst happen to you, being a mouse isn't really so bad!

Little boys have to go to school. Mice don't. Mice don't have to pass exams. Mice don't have to worry about money. Mice, as far as I can see, have only two enemies, humans and cats. My grandmother is a human, but I know for certain that she will always love me whoever I am. And she never, thank goodness, keeps a cat. When mice grow up, they don't ever have to go to war and fight against other mice. Mice, I felt pretty certain, all like each other. People don't.

Yes, I told myself, I don't think it is at all a bad thing to be a mouse.

Draw a portrait of yourself as a mouse.

What would your life be like if you were a mouse instead of a person?

_____

_____

_____

_____

_____

_____

_____

_____

_____

THE ANCIENT ONES

Four of the ancient witches meet in The Grand High Witch's hotel room to pick up their personal bottles of Delayed Action Mouse-Maker. But they are so old, they can't even remember each other's names! Using the clues below, figure out each witch's name, her age, and her favorite trick to make a child disappear.

		NAME				AGE			
		ETHEL	ROSEMARY	THELMA	GERTRUDE	86	90	94	98
TRICK	HAMBURGER								
	SNAIL								
	STONE								
	RABBIT								
AGE	86								
	90								
	94								
	98								

TIP: Each box represents a spot where two of the witch's traits match up. If you figure out that two of the traits go together, put an O in the box where they meet. If the traits don't match up, put an X in the box to rule it out. Use logic and reasoning to eliminate all the wrong answers until you get to the right one! If you get stuck, check the bottom of the page for another hint.

CLUES

1. Rosemary is 94 years old.
2. Ethel is younger than Rosemary.
3. Ethel and Gertrude like to turn children into living creatures.
4. The oldest witch likes turning children into snails, while the youngest likes to turn them into stones.

Hint: Thelma is younger than Ethel.

SCRAMBLED WITCHES

Unscramble the words and phrases below. See how many you can figure out without using hints!

1. **SORP GONGSPIDD** _ _ _ _ ' _ _ _ _ _ _ _ _ _ _

2. **OCACARELT HOB** _ _ _ _ _ _ _ _ _ _ _ _ _

3. **SALCW** _ _ _ _ _ _

4. **RESICE ESCOYTT** _ _ _ _ _ _ _ _ _ _ _ _ _

5. **CINERLHD** _ _ _ _ _ _ _ _ _

6. **WESTS PHESO** _ _ _ _ _ _ _ _ _ _ _

7. **IMCGA** _ _ _ _ _

1. Hint: Don't bathe too often
2. Hint: A sweet treat that might contain Formula 86 Delayed Action Mouse-Maker
3. Hint: Why witches wear gloves
4. Hint: Every country has one of these witch groups
5. Hint: Witches hate them
6. Hint: Avoid eating anything from these places
7. Hint: A witch's greatest weapon

A VITCH WHO DARES TO SAY I'M WRONG . . .

Quick! Solve the puzzle if you don't want The Grand High Witch to frizzle you like a fritter or cook you like a carrot.

ACROSS

2. My white mice were named Mary and _____.

3. If you don't want witches to smell you, it's best to avoid taking one of these.

5. My grandmother made me a mouse toothbrush out of this.

9. One of the cooks cut this part of my body in the kitchen.

10. A witch's nostrils are curvy like the inside of one of these.

11. This boy was turned into a statue by the witches.

13. I poured the Mouse-Maker into this food to beat the witches.

15. Formula 86 Delayed Action Mouse-Maker is this color.

16. The Grand High Witch has a machine that can create as much of this as she wants.

DOWN

1. My grandmother almost always has one of these in her hand.

4. The witches' meeting was held in one of these.

6. The witches pretended to be from the Royal Society for the Prevention of _____ to Children.

7. To make Formula 86 Delayed Action Mouse-Maker, you must boil the wrong end of this instrument.

8. I taught my pet mice to walk across one of these for my White Mouse Circus.

12. This greedy boy was turned into a mouse by the witches.

14. The Grand High Witch's castle is in this country.

A GREAT ESCAPE

I saw my chance. I jumped out from behind the bedpost and ran like lightning towards the open door. I jumped over several pairs of shoes on the way and in three seconds I was out in the corridor, still clutching the precious bottle to my chest.

Quick! Bring the bottle of Mouse-Maker from The Grand High Witch's hotel room back to Grandmother's room without being caught by Mr. Stringer or the maid. Follow the maze to safety!

THE TRIUMPH

Suddenly all the other witches, more than eighty of them, were beginning to scream and jump up out of their seats as though spikes were being stuck into their bottoms. Some were standing on chairs, some were up on the tables, and all of them were wiggling about and waving their arms in the most extraordinary manner.

In another few seconds, all the witches had completely disappeared and the tops of the two long tables were swarming with small brown mice.

Fill in the speech balloons with what you imagine the witches might be shouting as they turn into mice!

COUNT THE MICE!

MEMORY GAME

To catch a witch, you need to have a sharp mind! Use the stickers in the back of this book to create your own witch-themed memory game. This game works best with two or three players, but it can be fun to practice your memory skills alone, too.

You will need

A ruler
A pencil
Cardboard or heavy paper
Scissors
12 pairs of matching stickers, from this book

INSTRUCTIONS

1. Using a ruler and a pencil, draw 24 squares (about 2 inches on each side) on a piece of cardboard or heavy paper.
2. With help from an adult, cut out the squares. Be sure to make them all the same size, or the game won't work!
3. Put all 24 stickers from the back of this book onto the 24 squares of paper or cardboard, making 12 pairs of matching cards.

TO PLAY

1. Mix up all the cards and lay them facedown on a table or the floor.
2. Taking turns with the other player(s), flip two of the cards faceup. If they are a match, take both cards out of the game and put them in your scoring pile. If they are not a match, flip them back over and move to the next player.
3. Keep taking turns until all the pairs have been found. The player with the most pairs in their scoring pile is the winner!

If you want to make a bigger deck so more people can play, you can add as many other pairs of cards as you like by drawing pictures on more cards or using other matching stickers.

AROUND THE WORLD

"After that, my darling, the greatest task of all will begin for you and me! We shall pack our bags and go travelling all over the world! In every country we visit, we shall seek out the houses where the witches are living! It will be a triumph, my darling!"

In order to travel around the world, eliminating all the witches, you'll need to be able to speak a few other languages.

Match the different translations of the word *witch* to the correct language.

bruja	Greek
sorcière	Estonian
noita	Chinese
μάγισσα	Italian
boszorkány	Hungarian
mchawi	Japanese
bruxa	Finnish
Hexe	French
mụ phù thủy	Welsh
nõid	Swahili
strega	Portuguese
gwrach	Norwegian
まじょ	Spanish
巫婆	Vietnamese
heks	German

ANSWER KEY

PAGE 7

PAGE 22
Ethel, Rabbit, 90
Rosemary, Hamburger, 94
Thelma, Stone, 86
Gertrude, Snail, 98

PAGE 23
1. DOGS' DROPPINGS
2. CHOCOLATE BAR
3. CLAWS
4. SECRET SOCIETY
5. CHILDREN
6. SWEET SHOPS
7. MAGIC

PAGES 24-25

Across and down crossword solution:
- 2. WILLIAM
- 3. BATH
- 5. MATCHSTICK
- 9. TAIL
- 10. SEASHELL
- 11. HARALD
- 13. SOUP
- 15. GREEN
- 16. MONEY
- 1. CIGAR
- 4. HOTEL
- 6. CRUELTY
- 7. TELESCOOP
- 12. BRUNO
- 14. NORWAY

PAGE 26

PAGES 28-29
47

PAGE 31
bruja = Spanish
sorcière = French
noita = Finnish
μάγισσα = Greek
boszorkány = Hungarian
mchawi = Swahili
bruxa = Portuguese
Hexe = German
mụ phù thủy = Vietnamese
nõid = Estonian
strega = Italian
gwrach = Welsh
まじょ = Japanese
巫婆 = Chinese
heks = Norwegian

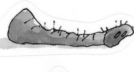

CHEESE

SNIPPY-SNIP

CRACK AND SNAP

PAGES 18-19 | GUZZLING SVEETS | A TRRRICE | VITCH'S EAR

CHILDREN | SCHOOLS | MICE | TWO FEET

FRY | GRRROWING FUR | SCHOOL-RRROOM | VOT'S GOING ON?

SQVISH THEM | FRRREAKS | TEACHERS | HALF-PAST NINE

MAGIC POWDER | VISKERS | GET OUT | RRREAD

'EAT UP!' | TINY LEGS | MOUSE-TRRRAPS | SHOUT HOORAY